Shipwreck

Carmel Reilly
Samantha Asri and Stevie Mahardhika

Australia • Brazil • Japan • Korea • Mexico • Singapore • Spain • United Kingdom • United States

Shipwreck

Fast Forward
Silver Level 24

Text: Carmel Reilly
Illustrations: Samantha Asri and Stevie Mahardhika
Editor: Cameron Macintosh
Design: Mandi Cole
Series design: James Lowe
Production controller: Seona Galbally
Audio recordings: Juliet Hill, Picture Start
Spoken by: Matthew King and Abbe Holmes
Reprint: Siew Han Ong

ISBN 978 0 17 012706 6
ISBN 978 0 17 012705 9 (set)

Cengage Learning Australia
Level 7, 80 Dorcas Street
South Melbourne, Victoria Australia 3205
Phone: 1300 790 853

Cengage Learning New Zealand
Unit 4B Rosedale Office Park
331 Rosedale Road, Albany, North Shore NZ 0632
Phone: 0508 635 766

For learning solutions, visit cengage.com.au

Printed in Australia by Ligare Pty Ltd
6 7 8 9 10 11 12 21 20 19 18 17

Evaluated in independent research by staff from the Department of Language, Literacy and Arts Education at the University of Melbourne.

Shipwreck

Carmel Reilly
Samantha Asri and Stevie Mahardhika

MILLY AND MATT COULDN'T WAIT TO LEAVE. THEY'D BEEN SAILING MANY TIMES WITH THEIR PARENTS, BUT THIS TIME WAS DIFFERENT. THEIR FATHER HAD BUILT HIS DREAM YACHT. NOW, HE TOLD THEM, THEY COULD SAIL AROUND THE WORLD IN STYLE. THIS WAS GOING TO BE THE ADVENTURE OF A LIFETIME.

THE DAY THE FAMILY LEFT PORT WAS WARM AND SUNNY. FOR THE FIRST FIVE DAYS, THEY WERE LUCKY – THE WEATHER STAYED FINE, AND THE SEA WAS CALM. THERE WAS JUST ENOUGH BREEZE TO FILL THE SAILS.

BY THE TIME NIGHT FELL, THE YACHT STARTED TO ROLL WILDLY.

THE NEXT MORNING ...
MILLY! MILLY! ARE YOU OKAY?
I THINK SO ... WHERE ARE WE?
I DON'T KNOW.
MUM AND DAD?!
THEY WERE IN THE OTHER LIFE RAFT. I SAW THEM JUST AFTER THE YACHT WENT DOWN, BUT ...

Running Words 230

HEY, MATT, DON'T DRINK IT ALL.
SORRY.
THERE'S NOT MUCH LEFT!
IT LOOKS LIKE WE MIGHT BE IN LUCK.
I THINK THERE'S A STREAM.
WE CAN GET MORE WATER.

THEY FILL THEIR WATER BOTTLES AT THE STREAM, AND LOOK FURTHER DOWN THE BEACH.
I MIGHT BE ABLE TO SEE SOMETHING IF I CLIMB UP ONTO THOSE ROCKS.
WHAT CAN YOU SEE?
NOTHING! JUST ONE LONG BEACH. NO SIGN OF LIFE.
IT'LL BE DARK SOON. LET'S GO BACK AND EAT SOME MORE CRACKERS.

BACK AT THE RAFT ...
HEY, DID YOU EAT MORE OF THOSE CRACKERS? THE OPEN PACKET HAS GONE.
I THINK WE ATE THEM BEFORE.
HEY, THERE'S SOME GOOD STUFF IN HERE.
MILLY USES THE NET TO CATCH A FISH. MATT MAKES A FIRE WITH DRIFTWOOD.
I KNEW GIRL SCOUT TRAINING WOULD COME IN HANDY ONE DAY!

THE NEXT MORNING ...
I COULDN'T SLEEP LAST NIGHT. IT FELT LIKE SOMEONE WAS WATCHING US.
I'M SURE IT WAS JUST A DREAM.
MATT!! DID YOU EAT THE REST OF THE FISH?
NO.
MAYBE YOU WEREN'T DREAMING. I THINK SOMEONE'S STEALING OUR FOOD.
I TOLD YOU WE WERE BEING WATCHED!
I GUESS AT LEAST IT MEANS WE'RE NOT ALONE ...
BUT IS THAT GOOD OR BAD?

MILLY AND MATT SET OFF TO LOOK FOR MUM AND DAD.
IT FEELS LIKE WE'VE BEEN WALKING FOREVER.
LET'S STOP FOR THE NIGHT WHEN WE GET AROUND THOSE ROCKS.

THE ROCKS ARE DIFFICULT TO CLIMB OVER.
WHOA!
I THOUGHT I WAS GOING TO LOSE YOU.
AS IF YOU COULD EVER LOSE ME!

FINALLY, AFTER WALKING FOR MANY HOURS ...
HEY, I CAN SEE SOMETHING!
JUST WAIT UNTIL WE GET A BIT CLOSER.
LOOK, IT'S A WASHED-UP LIFE RAFT. BUT WHAT IS THAT?
IT LOOKS LIKE A SHIRT TIED TO A POLE.

IT'S DAD'S SHIRT!
MUM AND DAD MUST HAVE LEFT IT AS A SIGN.
BUT WHERE DID THEY GO?
THEY'RE PROBABLY LOOKING FOR US, LIKE WE'RE LOOKING FOR THEM.
ALL WE CAN DO NOW IS WAIT HERE FOR THE NIGHT.
AND, HEY, WE'VE GOT COCONUT AND CRACKERS FOR DINNER AGAIN. WOO HOO!

THE NEXT MORNING ...
HEY, MATT. LOOK, AN ARROW! WE DIDN'T SEE IT LAST NIGHT IN THE DARK.
THEY WANT US TO GO THAT WAY ... INTO THE JUNGLE!
IT'S DARK IN HERE, BUT THERE SEEMS TO BE A TRACK.
I DON'T LIKE THIS.
LOOK! IT'S A PIECE OF DAD'S SHIRT TIED TO A BRANCH. WE'RE GOING THE RIGHT WAY.

LATER ...
HEY, LOOK! HERE'S ANOTHER PIECE OF DAD'S SHIRT.
STOP, MILLY. CAN'T YOU HEAR THOSE NOISES?
LOOK, I CAN SEE A CLEARING IN THE TREES.
WAIT! WE DON'T KNOW WHO'S UP THERE. JUST TAKE IT EASY.
BUT MILLY, IT'S GOT TO BE THEM.
DOES IT, MATT? THERE'S SOMEONE ELSE HERE. THEY'VE BEEN STEALING OUR FOOD AND WATCHING US – AND THEY'RE NOT MUM AND DAD.

YOU'RE RIGHT.
LET'S JUST TAKE THIS EASY. OKAY?
HEY, WHAT'S THAT?
IT LOOKS LIKE ... IT LOOKS LIKE ...
IT LOOKS LIKE MONKEYS.
AND PEOPLE FEEDING THEM ...
PEOPLE, MATT. THERE ARE PEOPLE OVER THERE. REAL PEOPLE!

HEY, WHAT DO YOU KIDS THINK YOU'RE DOING?
LOOKING FOR OUR MUM AND DAD!

MATT AND MILLY SOON FIND THE POLICE STATION.

YOUR MUM AND DAD HAVE HIRED A LOCAL BOAT TO TAKE THEM OUT ALONG THE COAST LOOKING FOR YOU. LUCKY THE BOAT HAS A RADIO. THE CAPTAIN SAYS THEY'LL BE BACK IN 20 MINUTES.

THANK YOU SO MUCH!

20 MINUTES LATER ...

THANK GOODNESS!

MUM! DAD!

LATER THAT DAY ...
IT WAS GREAT THE WAY YOU LEFT THOSE SIGNS FOR US TO FOLLOW.
WE DIDN'T KNOW IF YOU'D SEE THEM ... WE JUST HOPED YOU'D SURVIVED.
WE DIDN'T KNOW ABOUT YOU EITHER, DAD.
YOU KNOW, IT WAS THE MONKEYS WHO SAVED US.
THE MONKEYS?

WE CAUGHT THEM STEALING OUR SUPPLIES.
I'D READ ABOUT THESE MONKEYS. I KNEW THEY LIVED ON THESE ISLANDS AND I KNEW THAT THEY MUST KNOW ENOUGH ABOUT HUMANS TO KNOW ABOUT OUR FOOD.
DAD THOUGHT THAT IF WE FOLLOWED THEM, THEY'D LEAD US TO PEOPLE.
I COULD HAVE BEEN WRONG. BUT, THANK GOODNESS, I WAS RIGHT.

SO, YOU WERE STEALING FROM US, TOO.
AND WATCHING US AS WE WALKED AROUND.
IT'S GOOD TO KNOW I WASN'T IMAGINING THINGS.
JUST FOR ONCE!
SO, WHAT ARE WE GOING TO DO NOW?
WELL, THAT'S WHAT WE WANTED TO TALK TO YOU ABOUT ...

TWO WEEKS LATER ...
I STILL CAN'T BELIEVE WE'VE BOUGHT A NEW BOAT.
I CAN'T BELIEVE WE'RE GOING TO SAIL HOME IN IT!
JUST ONE THING.
WHAT?
NO MORE CRACKERS. BREAKFAST BARS, DRIED FRUIT, NUTS ... THEY'RE ALL OK. BUT NO MORE CRACKERS!